HEAR MY ROAR
A STORY OF FAMILY VIOLENCE

Written by Dr. Ty Hochban
Illustrated by Vladyana Krykorka

Annick Press Ltd.
Toronto • New York

To ending family violence.

T.H.

To Dr. D.E. for her empathy and support.

V.K.

©1994 Ty Hochban (text)
©1994 Vladyana Krykorka (art)
Design by Vladyana Krykorka.

Annick Press Ltd.

Annick Press gratefully acknowledges the support of the Canada Council and the Ontario Arts Council.

Acknowledgements

The Afterword was written by the Health Programs and Services Branch of Health Canada. The publisher would like to thank them for their valuable contributions to the development of this book. Special thanks to Lina Calamo for her commitment to seeing the project through.

The publisher also wishes to thank the Kids Help Phone. Kids Help Phone is a Canadian, toll-free, confidential service available to children like Lungin, but is also for any young person who has a problem or question they need help with. **Call 1-800-668-6868 (Canada only).**

Canadian Cataloguing in Publication Data
Hochban, Ty
Hear my roar: a story of family violence

ISBN 1-55037-969-0

1. Family violence - Juvenile literature.
2. Family violence - Prevention - Juvenile literature.
3. Victims of family violence - Services for -
Juvenile literature. I. Krykorka, Vladyana. II. Title.

HQ809.H63 1994   j362.82'92   C93-095274-X

The art in this book was rendered in pen and ink. The text was typeset in Bodoni Book.

Distributed in Canada by:
Firefly Books Ltd.
250 Sparks Ave.
Willowdale, ON M2H 2S4

Published in the U.S.A. by Annick Press (U.S.) Ltd.
Distributed in the U.S.A. by:
Firefly Books (U.S.) Inc.
P.O. Box 1338
Ellicott Station
Buffalo, NY 14205

Printed and bound in Canada by Metropole Litho, Quebec.

Many women and children experience violence in the home on a regular basis. This book is intended to help children who have been exposed to family violence. It is meant to act as a framework for discussing feelings and challenging the idea of violence as a way of controlling other people.

Hear my Roar *is the story of a family in which the father becomes abusive towards the mother and their child. The mother becomes concerned when she realizes what effect the violence is having on the family. She asks for help from her family doctor and takes action towards ending the abuse.*

The story ends with the mother, Anna, and her son, Lungin, leaving to visit a shelter as their first step in developing their new life together. The father, Orsa, begins to acknowledge his responsibility for the violence and is offered help for his problem.

Children learn by watching the behaviour of family members and friends. If they see people using violence "successfully" as a way of solving problems, they might adopt that behaviour as well. Children in violent homes can suffer anxiety, fear, and even physical injury in the short term, and behavioural and emotional problems in the long term. Children need to learn that violence in the family is never appropriate. It does not resolve conflicts and using it to control others is unacceptable. They must learn that violence does not have to be tolerated and that action can be taken to stop it.

All children must learn that the person committing the violence is responsible for his or her own behaviour. The violence is not the child's fault. They need to learn how to protect themselves when faced with violence and how to find help when they need it. Above all, children must learn that they are safe and loved by their caregivers. If you have any concerns regarding a child in your care or whom you know, I encourage you to contact someone who can help. This might be your family doctor, guidance counsellor, social worker, or anyone else you trust to help you take action.

Finally, a word of caution. If this book is kept in the home, and you believe your partner will disapprove, it might put you at risk of further violence. Be careful where you keep the book.

Reading the Book

You might find the following suggestions helpful when reading this book with a child. First, read the story through once to yourself, taking as much time as you need. You might see parallels to your own situation and want to highlight them for discussion.

When reading the book to a younger child, use the pictures to help tell the story. If the child is older, try to involve him or her more in the text and spend time discussing feelings and sharing ideas. And again, take your time. One purpose of this book is to provide you with an opportunity to spend some peaceful time together with a child. This is time to understand what has happened, talk, and to share plans and dreams for the future.

Since many children have difficulty focusing their attention for long periods of time, use rest breaks to avoid becoming frustrated. Try to find a quiet place with few distractions. This will improve your child's attention and provide you both with some much-needed peace.

Ty Hochban

CHAPTER ONE

**O**NCE UPON A TIME, in the woods by the shore, there lived a gentle small family of gentle small creatures.

Orsa is the father. See him there eating corn on the cob? Anna is the mother. That's her pouring tea. The small one's named Lungin. He has a ball.

It was summer and that meant there was all the food you could eat. After lunch they would play in the tall grass, or splash in the shallows of the stream.

Today they were going fishing. Orsa and Lungin stood on the rocks with their fishing poles. Anna prepared Lungin's lessons in the shade by the stream.

"Maybe I should give you two a lesson in fishing," she teased.

"Save your lessons for the boy, Anna," Orsa huffed. "We're just waiting for the biggest fish so there will be fewer for you to clean."

"Oh, no, Orsa," Anna laughed. "You know the rules. You catch 'em, you clean 'em."

"Lungin, when we used to hunt," Orsa said, "before we knew how to grow our own food, we roared to scare the animals into our traps. Let me hear you roar." Lungin filled his tiny cheeks with air and let out his tiny roar.

"Ho ho, that's not a roar. Now try it like this," Orsa said, and he filled his great chest and roared a tremendous "ROAR!"

Lungin jumped up and down (and nearly out of his skin), and they laughed and roared the whole afternoon. Anna smiled as she watched them both showing off and covered her ears when their roars got too loud.

Day by day, the summer rolled along and the whole family worked together in the warm summer sun. Orsa would collect wood and help Anna with the garden. Anna passed on to Lungin her knowledge of the forest.

Lungin studied his lessons and helped his parents with the chores. He learned all about the forest and the sea. He learned which plants are good to eat, and which can make you sick. He studied very hard.

CHAPTER TWO

**T**HE WARM summer days grew shorter, and soon it was fall. The leaves changed colour and the wind raced the birds south for the winter.

Fall arrived much earlier this year and caught the family unprepared for the coming winter. The cold windy weather dried out the berries and blew away the twigs they needed for firewood. Lungin and his parents worked hard to get ready for the winter. They were cold and hungry and very, very tired. On the coldest nights they would share a cup of Jackberry wine to warm their empty bellies. Orsa would take an extra sip from the bottle before putting it away. "One for the Sandman," he'd say with a wink. Anna and Orsa argued more often in the cold autumn nights. Lungin missed the summer.

Just before the first snow, Lungin was tucked into bed with kisses and wishes for magical dreams, a good winter's sleep, and another happy summer when they all woke up in the spring.

Orsa and Anna gathered up the last of the food, shut the doors and windows, and settled into their own beds for the winter.

"I'm sorry I've been so cross lately, Anna," Orsa said quietly, "but when we wake up in the spring everything will be fine."

"I know, Orsa," Anna said. "I'm sure all we need is a good winter's sleep." She kissed Orsa on the ear and whispered, "I love you."

"I love you too, Anna," Orsa said, as he rolled over and fell into a restless, troubled sleep.

Throughout the long, cold winter they slept and dreamed.

Lungin dreamed of rolling in the hills and eating great piles of fresh berries. He dreamed of his father throwing him high in the air, and flying all around the forest.

From high up in the trees he heard his father roaring and growling and saw his mother gathering herbs. Anna was covering her ears and calling for him to come down as he flew higher and higher in the forest of his dreams.

Wrapped tight in her blanket, Anna dreamed of the first time she met Orsa, many years ago. He was tall and strong and gentle and kind. He made her feel happier than she had ever felt before.

Then she dreamed that she was walking through the snow with Lungin. They were looking for Orsa, but couldn't find him anywhere. She heard a monster roaring and growling and chasing them through her dreams. They ran and ran through the snow, with the monster close behind.

Orsa tossed and turned the whole winter long. He dreamed that he looked into a pool and saw an evil, angry face staring back at him. When he roared out for help, everyone ran away. In his dream, everything he touched broke or died, and this made him feel even more frightened, more angry, and more alone.

CHAPTER THREE

NNA AND ORSA
woke up to get the house ready for the spring, but when they looked outside it made their hearts shiver.

"It's still so cold and wet," Anna said, discouraged. "We need to find food and dry wood, and clean up all this mess. Oh, why couldn't we wake up to a warm, sunny morning."

"You clean up the mess and I'll go see what I can find," Orsa said, and stomped off into the trees.

Anna went about clearing away the leaves and twigs from the yard, swept out the house and picked some fresh spring flowers.

"Orsa will feel better when he sees everything so clean and has something to eat," she told herself. "All we need is some good luck and a little peace and everything will be fine."

Orsa came back shivering and growling, "Grrr, no fruit, no wood, and this cold, wet wind! Grrr!"

"Orsa, come rest and have something to eat," Anna said, trying to sound happy. "You'll feel better after you've eaten."

"These are the same dried berries we have all the time. I'd rather go hungry than eat those mouldy old berries," Orsa said, and knocked everything off the table and stormed into the house.

"Orsa, please! That's all the food we have. Please don't be angry," Anna said, but Orsa was off into the house before she could stop him. She wrapped her shawl around her shoulders, ran behind the house, and felt so upset that she cried and cried.

"Oh, now what have I done? What can I do?" Anna wept

quietly. "I'm cold and hungry too, and my ears won't stop ringing." After a few minutes she thought, "I have to find some food and build a nice warm fire," and sniffed away the last of the tears. "I'm glad Lungin is still sleeping. Such a scene would have given him an awful fright." She bundled herself up and hurried off into the woods.

But from under his blanket, on the other side of the wall, Lungin had been listening to his mother crying. He shivered a little, then curled up in his bed, and after tossing and turning fell back to sleep.

Soon Anna was back with wood for the fire and an armful of roots to cook for dinner. "These will make a good hot meal," she said to herself, finishing the stew. Orsa came out to find Anna stirring a big pot of roots and dried berries.

"That looks good, Anna. Where did you find all this food?" Orsa asked. "I'm so hungry I could eat acorns." Anna could tell he'd been drinking the Jackberry wine.

"Well, if we waited for you we would be eating acorns instead of Rootaberry stew," Anna answered sternly. "Now sit down and eat so we can get back to work." She felt good because she had done so well that day to find food and wood. She was upset that Orsa had wasted the day drinking, but she was glad he wasn't angry anymore.

After dinner Anna cleaned up the dishes and put away the extra food. Orsa sat on his favourite stone and drank and drank until he was silly and drunk and stumbling around.

"Anna," Orsa roared, waving his bottle in the air, "wake up Lungin so he can help me with the work."

"Let him sleep, Orsa. He needs his rest if he's going to grow," Anna answered carefully. "I don't want him to see you drunk like this."

"Roar! I'll tell you when I'm drunk, and I say wake him up," Orsa bellowed. Anna was so scared that she covered her ears and ran into the house.

She went into Lungin's room where he was pretending to be asleep. "Lungin, it's time to get up. I want to talk to you," she said softly.

"Yes, Mother," Lungin said, stretching, and rubbing his eyes.

"Lungin, it's spring now and your father thinks that you should be up to help with the chores," Anna said. "Baby, you must promise to behave. Your father is very tired and worried and I don't want you to upset him." Anna gave him a hug and helped him get washed, and they went out to go to work on his lessons.

Orsa was snoring when Anna came out, and she gave a small sigh of relief.

"What's wrong with Daddy? Is he sick?" Lungin asked.

"No, he's just sleeping, dear. He's been working very hard today," Anna answered. "Come on now. Let's go before we wake him up." But Lungin saw the bottle of Jackberry wine, and he knew why his father was sleeping so soundly.

CHAPTER FOUR

HE EARLY WEEKS
of spring passed. The days became warmer and the food easier
to find, but the problems at home continued. Orsa was getting
meaner and louder every day, and nothing Anna could do
would make him happy.

Sometimes he would apologize after getting angry, then
everything would be fine for awhile. He would be happy and
kind to Anna and Lungin and they loved these warm times
together. Then, without any warning, it would all start again.

He spent many nights drinking and roaring and crashing
around the house. He slept late into the afternoon while Anna
worked in the garden and Lungin worked on his lessons.

He smashed the dishes if he didn't like the food and he tore
up Lungin's lessons if he made a mistake. Anna was so upset
from all the roaring and fighting that she couldn't eat or sleep.

Anna knew all this was bad for Lungin, but she never knew
how bad until one day when she found him playing with his
dolls.

"Give me some bread! I'm hungry," he said for the papa doll.

"We're all out of bread," he answered for the mama doll.

"Roar! Then get some more or I'll roar so loud I'll split your ears," and he grabbed up the mama doll and shook it in the air. "Do this! Do that! Do it or I'll smash you!"

"Where's the baby doll, Lungin?" Anna asked over his shoulder. Lungin was surprised.

"Over here," he said softly. He lifted up a leaf and showed her the tiny baby doll hiding underneath.

"Why is he hiding?" Anna asked.

"He's scared because he ate the bread and now Daddy's mad," he said.

"Is he hiding from Mommy, too?" Anna asked.

"Yes. She says Baby's bad because he won't do his lessons," Lungin pouted. "And he's mad at her because she won't stop the fighting."

After that day Anna watched Lungin's behaviour more closely, and noticed many changes that she couldn't understand.

Sometimes he was quiet and shy, as though he was lost deep inside himself, or hiding a terrible secret.

Sometimes he acted like a bully and had temper tantrums if he didn't get his way.

And Anna had a hard time getting him to work on his lessons. He seemed too nervous or excited to concentrate.

Lungin was having headaches and tummy aches nearly every day, and Anna wondered if he might be sick. She decided it was time to go see Dr. Woodland.

CHAPTER FIVE

HE NEXT MORNING, Anna and Lungin got up early and set off on their long walk to the doctor's house in the hills. Orsa was still asleep and Anna was careful not to wake him. Anna and Lungin washed up quietly, packed lunch, and closed the door softly behind them.

"Why do we have to be so quiet, Mom? Don't you want to wake Daddy?" Lungin whispered as they left the house.

"Everything makes Orsa so angry lately. I think it's best if we keep this visit to the doctor a secret for now," Anna answered. "I left him a note that said we've gone to the beach to look for shells."

On their long walk they watched the birds in the air, the leaves blowing in the breeze, and the bugs crawling along the ground. Soon they were high in the hills, walking up the path to the doctor's house.

"Mom, I'm scared. What's going to happen? Is this going to hurt?" Lungin was full of questions.

"Don't worry, Lungin," Anna answered. "I first met Dr. Woodland when I was small, like you. We had a nice visit, and I left feeling much better. This doctor is easy to talk to," she said, a little nervous herself as she knocked on the tiny door.

"Hello, hello, hello out there. Come around the back. I'm working by the fire." They followed the path around the house and saw the doctor stirring a boiling pot on a crackling fire.

"Hello, Anna," Dr. Woodland said, "and this must be Lungin. Come along and have a seat. Now what brings you all the way up here? The last time I saw you was when this young fellow was born. And look how big he is now," the doctor said with a smile.

"Well, ever since springtime, Lungin has been having stomachaches and headaches, and he just hasn't been himself," Anna said. "And my ears have been ringing and hurting all summer long. What do you think the trouble is?"

"Let's take a look at you and see what we can find," Dr. Woodland said, and started to examine them.

The doctor looked in their eyes with bright lights, and peeked in their ears. Lungin was told to say "ahh" and his belly was poked and jiggled. He wasn't scared anymore, as the doctor laughed and talked and checked them both over from head to toe.

"Anna, your ears look okay, and I can't find anything wrong with Lungin. Is there anything else wrong that might explain all this trouble?" Dr. Woodland asked quietly.

"Well," Anna answered slowly, "things haven't been going very well at home lately."

"I see... Anna, listen, let's go sit down and talk over a nice cup of tea. Lungin, could you stay out here and watch my kettle? I want to talk to your mother inside."

"Okay." Lungin waved to them as he warmed his feet by the fire.

Anna and Dr. Woodland sat inside and talked. Anna described how angry and mean Orsa had been all summer. The doctor sat and listened while Anna poured out all the things she'd been holding inside. She cried sometimes as she talked about everything that had happened.

"I just don't know what to do anymore. Everything I do just makes him more angry. I try so hard, but I just can't do anything right. Some days he's fine, just like he used to be. He says he's sorry for getting angry and then treats us very well. I feel like I must be to blame. But I get so scared sometimes that I can't eat or sleep, and Orsa roars so loud I think my ears will burst," Anna cried.

"Anna, I'm glad you came to talk to me. I want you to know that I believe what you're saying and I want to help," Dr. Woodland said. "Now tell me a little more about Lungin."

They talked a little longer. Then Anna went out to call Lungin.

"Come in, Lungin," she said. "The doctor wants to talk with you." Lungin came in and Dr. Woodland came over, speaking to him in a soft voice.

"Lungin, your mother has been telling me about all the trouble at home and all the smashing-up of things. Would you like to tell me about it?" Lungin looked up at his mother, and she put her hand on his shoulder and nodded.

"Sometimes I think we make him mad, so he roars or hits us," he said. "I try to do better, but sometimes he gets angry anyway."

"Okay," said the doctor, and looked at them both with soft blue eyes. "I'm going to tell you something before we go on, and it's very important." Anna and Lungin listened closely.

"When Orsa yells, or smashes things, or hits you when he's angry, it is not your fault. It's wrong to hit, and it's wrong to hurt, and he has nobody to blame but himself." Dr. Woodland gave them a gentle smile. "I want you to tell me more about what's been going on at home, but this is something that I want you to remember, okay?"

Anna and Lungin nodded and Lungin felt his mother give him a hug. For the first time all summer, he started to feel safe.

"Now, let me get you both a hot cup of tea and we can talk some more. I'm very happy you came to see me today," the doctor said with another smile, and went back out to the fire.

"How does your stomach feel now?" Anna asked.

"Nice and quiet," Lungin answered, a little surprised. "How about your ears?"

Anna smiled and squeezed his hand.

"Better, Lungin, much better."

Dr. Woodland came back with three cups of tea and they talked together for the rest of the afternoon.

"Oh my," Anna said suddenly. "I didn't realize it was so late. We have to get back home or Orsa will be very angry."

"I understand. If you need any more help I want you to come back," said the doctor, as they walked back to the path.

On their long walk home, Anna and Lungin talked about all the things Dr. Woodland had said. "Tell me what you remember," Anna said. Lungin thought for a minute and started counting on his fingers:

- Hitting and shouting and hurting are wrong.
- When Daddy gets mad and hurts us, it's his fault, not ours.
- If I think he's going to start hitting, I should hide or go to a safe place.
- If I find a telephone, I can call the emergency number.

"That's good, Lungin," Anna said, with a hug and a kiss on his head. "And when we get home and your father's not around, I'll pack a bag with some clothes and a little money. I'll hide it in the house in case we have to leave in a hurry."

Knowing these things made Anna and Lungin feel much safer, and Anna felt better having talked about why Lungin was behaving so strangely.

"Lungin, I never knew you had seen so much of our fighting," Anna said. "I'm sorry we didn't look for help sooner."

"I know you were scared and trying to keep everyone happy," Lungin answered. "I was scared, too."

"I love you, Lungin, and I'm very proud of you. Now let's get home quickly. We're not out of the woods yet," Anna said, and they hurried down the path back home.

When Anna and Lungin got back it was already dark, and Orsa was snoring on his rock under the warm summer stars.

Lungin was off to sleep before Anna finished tucking him in, and she quietly went off to her own bed for the night. In the silent summer darkness, Anna's thoughts buzzed around like fireflies. "Oh, please let us find some peace," she said in a tiny, tired voice, and drifted off into a deep, dreamless sleep.

The next morning, Anna packed a small bag and hid it behind the house before she started making breakfast. Her heart was beating fast, but she felt better once everything was ready.

Lungin woke up and came out rubbing his eyes and stretching. "Are you hungry, sleepyhead?" Anna asked with a smile.

Lungin smiled back. "I'm starving, Mom," he said, and they both sat down for breakfast.

Soon Orsa came out and gave them a long, low growl. "Where were you two all day yesterday?"

"Looking for shells, Orsa, but we couldn't find any," Anna said. She felt bad about lying, but she knew Orsa wouldn't like her going to the doctor. "Come sit down and eat your breakfast."

"No thanks, Anna. No time to eat," he said with a grin, and clapped his hands together. "Lungin, hurry up and get some wood. We're going to make more wine today."

"Yes, Father," Lungin answered, looking down at his plate.

All morning long they worked at making wine. Anna and Lungin brought berries and wood, and Orsa stirred and tasted the wine.

"Orsa, we should save some berries for winter. Remember last year," Anna said carefully.

"There's plenty for winter. We need these for the wine," Orsa said with another gulp. "Lungin, more wood! We need a bigger fire."

"But, Dad, I just brought in some wood," Lungin laughed. Orsa grabbed him by the scruff of the neck and pushed him out the door.

"Orsa, no! You'll hurt him," Anna cried.

"I said more wood and I mean it," Orsa roared, and started throwing more sticks on the fire.

Lungin was scared. "I'd better hide outside and wait for Mom," he told himself, and ran around the back of the house.

"Orsa, you're getting drunk and the fire is too big," Anna cried. "Please stop and calm down."

Orsa looked at Anna with fierce red eyes. "Get back and leave me alone," he roared, and slapped her so hard it knocked her down!

"Orsa, no!" Anna yelled, and ran out of the house.

"Come back here," he roared, kicking over the fire and burning his foot. "ROAR!"

Anna found Lungin behind the house, grabbed the bag she'd hidden, and hurried off into the woods. "Lungin, quick, we have to run! We have to get back to Dr. Woodland."

"But, Mom, what about Dad?" Lungin cried. "I think he's hurt." Anna looked back and saw Orsa staggering around outside the burning house, roaring and waving his fists in the air.

"He's all right, Lungin. Are you okay? Did he hurt you?" Anna asked, and off they went.

"A little, Mom, but I'm okay," Lungin answered. "Where will we go now? We can't go home."

"We'll go see the doctor. We'll be all right there," Anna said, with Orsa's roars fading in the distance behind them.

When they arrived, Dr. Woodland invited them in to rest and describe what had happened.

"I'm sorry to hear about all this, Anna," the doctor said softly. "And I think you're right. You can't go back home now. I have some friends at a shelter where you can stay for awhile. They'll make sure you're safe and help you sort things out. I'll go see Orsa to make sure he's all right. He's going to need a lot of help to stop his roaring and drinking."

The doctor told them that the people at the shelter were expecting them, and showed them the way.

"Lungin," said Dr. Woodland, "I want you to know that your father loves you very much, but he has a serious problem controlling his temper. He needs help and time if he's going to stop all this hurting. Do you understand?"

"I think so," Lungin said. He was sad because he loved his father and he knew he wouldn't see him for a long time.

"I'll explain things to him," Anna said, putting her arm around Lungin. "Thank you for all your help."

That afternoon, Dr. Woodland went to see Orsa and found him sitting outside the burned-down house. "Hello, Orsa," said the doctor, coming up the path.

"Oh, hello, Doc. What are you doing here?" Orsa asked, surprised to see the doctor.

"I wanted you to know that Anna and Lungin are safe and staying with some friends of mine," Dr. Woodland said.

"Will you take me to them?" Orsa asked.

"No, Orsa," the doctor said, "you have got a problem with your temper and your drinking. You're going to have to get some help before you can see them again."

"I don't have a problem and I don't need your help," Orsa snapped, and he stamped his burned foot on the ground. It really hurt, but he didn't want the doctor to see him cry.

"Well, how about letting me take a look at that burn?" Dr. Woodland asked. "You wouldn't want it to get infected."

"Yeah, okay, Doc," Orsa said sadly, looking over at the house that was still smoking from the fire. "You know I really do love them," he said quietly.

"I know you do, Orsa, and they know it, too. That's why they want you to get help," Dr. Woodland said, cleaning and bandaging Orsa's foot. And they talked about everything that had happened that long, sad summer.

AFTERWORD

Who is your Dr. Woodland? It could be a friend, a relative, a neighbour, a social worker, a health care professional, or anyone else you can confide in and trust. In your case, approaching your family doctor may not be an option. But the important thing is that you learn how to protect yourself and know who you personally can turn to for help. This knowledge is the first step towards securing a safe, stable and more fulfilling life for both you and your child.

Unfortunately, this process of healing can be emotionally draining and seemingly endless. Instead of the "long, sad summer" that Anna and Lungin lived through, you may have been subjected to violence for much longer. Breaking such an established pattern of abuse takes not only time but patience and hope.

In fact, your story may be different from Lungin's in a number of ways: the people helping you may not act the same way as the characters in the book; you may be confused over what to do, although it seemed so clear to Anna and Lungin what action they should take; and, unlike Orsa, who began to recognize he was hurting his family, maybe the abuser in your home is not even willing to admit that he or she has a problem.

This kind of denial is especially common when alcohol is involved. But alcohol and violence do not necessarily go hand-in-hand, and no one in your family should have to tolerate either situation. Being drunk or under the influence of alcohol in no way excuses violent or other abusive behaviour. Furthermore, there is no reason to cover up for the alcohol abuser so that others will not know he has a problem (or so that he will not lose his job). To do so only enables the alcohol abuser to go on with his drinking and to continue to victimize others with violent behaviour.

Although talking to a friend or neighbour may make you feel better, taking action is the best way to break an abusive situation. There are a number of organizations that can help you. If you are being abused, look in your local (or nearest city) telephone book for: women's transition house or shelter, battered women's support group, social service agency, distress centre, police, or other community service organizations that provide counselling and support. Please remember, although your circumstances may be different from those of other victims of violence, you all have one thing in common — the potential to find a solution.

The violence in your home is not your fault, and it's not your child's fault either. After reading this story we hope it has become clear — just as it did for Anna and Lungin - that the person committing the violence is the only one responsible for that abusive behaviour. After you have made the first move, you will have time to think and some helpful person to talk to. With these first steps towards change, you are on your way to taking charge of your life, one step at a time, and making well-considered decisions about your future course of action.

Health Programs & Services Branch
Health Canada